Barbie™
A Fashion Fairytale

A Panorama Sticker Storybook

Based on the original screenplay by Elise Allen
Adapted by Justine Fontes
Illustrated by Dynamo Limited

Special thanks to: Vicki Jaeger, Monica Okazaki, Kathleen Warner, Emily Kelly,
Sarah Quesenberry, Carla Alford, Julia Phelps, Tanya Mann, Rob Hudnut,
Shelley Dvi-Vardhana, Michelle Cogan, Greg Winters,
Taia Morley, and Dynamo Limited

Reader's Digest
Children's Books®

Pleasantville, New York • Montréal, Québec • Bath, United Kingdom

Even gorgeous movie stars have bad days—Barbie was fired from her new movie for disagreeing with the director! Instantly the Internet buzzed with gossip calling Barbie a diva.

Her friends suggested getting away, and Barbie knew just where to go: Paris, to visit her Aunt Millicent. Barbie's aunt was a designer with her own fashion house there. She and her dog Sequin took off for the city of lights!

Barbie fondly recalled the fabrics, frills, and friendly faces in Millicent's fashion house—and her creative aunt at the center of it all. Millicent was amazing as ever. But her situation had changed. "I didn't want to tell you over the phone, but I'm closing up shop!"

Her loyal assistant, Alice, explained, "Jacqueline's across the street has ruined us. She copies Millicent's designs then spends all her time and money promoting herself. So the press loves her."

Barbie sadly agreed to help her aunt and Alice pack up the shop.

In the attic, Alice showed Barbie an ancient wardrobe with a legend, "If you put a worthy design inside and recite a special rhyme, magical creatures appear that make clothes glow with flair," she read.

Barbie spotted a gown designed by Alice that certainly looked worthy of testing the legend.

The girls put the dress in the wardrobe, then chanted:

With inspiration, love, and care
Great fashions earn a glow of flair.
Some shimmer, glimmer, and some shine.
Bring life and sparkles every time.

Suddenly the wardrobe's doors burst open! The girls gasped at the now-glittery gown surrounded by three small sparkling Flairies named Shyne, Shimmer, and Glimmer. The Flairies had come to life in Millicent's fashion house, and it was the source of their powers.

Alice and Barbie tried to convince Aunt Millicent not to sell. But it was too late! Millicent said, "To buy back the building I'd have to design and sell a whole new line in two days."

As soon as her aunt left, Barbie gave Alice a pep talk. With the help of the Flairies, the girls could create enough clothes to save the shop. They wasted no time getting to work!

When the two friends went out for a snack, Jacqueline and her assistant stole the Flairies and demanded that they glitterize Jacqueline's designs.

But the dull dresses didn't inspire the Flairies. They forced out some glitz, but Shyne warned that the magic wasn't stable.

Jacqueline didn't listen. She planned a fashion show for Friday.

Meanwhile at Millicent's, Alice panicked! "What can we do without the Flairies? They're missing!"

Barbie's aunt was awed by Alice's designs and offered to help. Alice was thrilled and flattered, especially when Millicent added, "I'm newly inspired by *you*."

With help from Sequin and Millicent's pets, the Flairies escaped in time to glitterize the clothes for the Fairy Tale Fashion Show. Ken, who came to Paris to surprise Barbie, even got some flair! Jacqueline's show was a huge flop. Millicent's show was a huge hit. And the guests bought more than enough fashions to save the shop!

To celebrate, Alice, Millicent, Barbie, and Ken attended an elegant ball. The Flairies even glitterized their ride!

Barbie no longer worried about what others thought of her. Because now she knew: As long as you stay true to your passion, you're bound to live happily ever after—and in style!